The Book of **Boys** (for Girls)

The Book of **Girls** (for Boys)

By David T. Greenberg   Illustrated by Joy Allen

LITTLE, BROWN AND COMPANY

New York ❧ Boston

Also by David T. Greenberg:

Bugs!

Skunks!

Slugs

Snakes!

Whatever Happened to Humpty Dumpty?

Also illustrated by Joy Allen:

Exploding Gravy

To Phyllis and John, the nicest girl and boy I know!
Love, David

To brother Jim and sister Cindie . . .
Our fun, fights, and friendship.
—J.A.

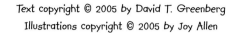

Text copyright © 2005 by David T. Greenberg
Illustrations copyright © 2005 by Joy Allen

Cheerios® is a registered trademark of General Mills.
Barbie® is a registered trademark of Mattel, Inc.

Little, Brown and Company

Time Warner Book Group
1271 Avenue of the Americas, New York, NY 10020
Visit our Web site at www.lb-kids.com

First Edition

Library of Congress Cataloging-in-Publication Data

Greenberg, David (David T.)
  The book of boys (for girls) & the book of girls (for boys) / by David T. Greenberg ; illustrated by Joy Allen.— 1st ed.
    p. cm.
  ISBN 0-316-36210-7 (hc)
  1. Sex differences (Psychology)—Juvenile poetry. 2. Children's poetry, American. 3. Girls—Juvenile poetry. 4. Boys—Juvenile poetry. I. Allen, Joy. II. Title.
PS3557.R37828B66 2005
811'.54—dc21

2002024008

10 9 8 7 6 5 4 3 2 1

Book design by Saho Fujii

SC

Manufactured in China

The illustrations for this book were done in watercolor and pencil on Fabriano Uno paper.
The text was set in Kidprint and General Collection-Cleanhouse,
and the display type was hand-lettered.

 What are little girls made of?
Sugar and spice and everything nice
That's what little girls are made of

 What are little boys made of?
Snips and snails and puppy dog tails
That's what little boys are made of

What is the reason for girls?
It's hard to understand
They're troublemaking squirrels
Girls should be banned

Why were boys invented?
Can anyone explain?
Boys are all demented
Boys are all a pain

They're always playing dress-ups
Wearing multicolored braces
Making awesome bathroom mess-ups
Sticking stickers on their faces

They're always playing in mud
Are covered with twigs and leaves
Chewing *bubble* gum like cud
Wiping boogers on their sleeves

They're made from sparkly fingernails
Gossiping? A lot!
Snips and snails and puppy dog tails?
Unquestionably not!

They're made from snakes and mice
Laundry starting to rot
Sugar and spice and everything nice?
Unquestionably not!

They're made from high-pitched shrieks
That will make your brain cells bubble
Putting lipstick on their beaks
AND GETTING BOYS IN TROUBLE!

They're made from untied sneaker laces
Bedrooms turned to rubble
Food stuck in their braces
AND GETTING GIRLS IN TROUBLE!

They'll lock the bathroom door
And refuse to let you in
You can beg, argue, roar
Yet all they do is grin

And girls have a smell
Like moldy chicken pie
That will make you feel unwell
Or possibly sicken, die

They'll steal the head off your Barbie doll
And stick it with a pin
You can plead, holler, bawl
Yet all they do is grin

And boys have got an aroma
Like liver juice and bacon
That will knock you into a coma
From which you'll never awaken

Girls will cause a fight to start
Say you're the one who started it
They'll sweetly smile, silently fart
Say you're the one who farted it

Boys cause girls to fight
Though they'll whine that it's not true
They'll fart out loud like dynamite
And blame the fart on you

Girls will trash your favorite coat
And factually say you did it
They'll say you lost the remote
When actually they hid it

Boys will hide the remote control
(Something they always deny)
They'll miss the toilet bowl
And forget to zip their fly

They'll dress the dog in people clothes
But yours are the clothes they use
They'll cover the kitchen with Cheerios
And you're the one they accuse

They'll make a tent from a blanket
But the blanket they use is yours!
Your lollipop, they'll yank it
They'll search through all of your drawers

So, what if girls push you
Tease you, treat you rough?
Just get up off your tush, you
Say you've had enough!

So, what if boys defy you?
Don't take it any longer
Just look them in the eye, you
And tell them that you're stronger

Yet some speculate
Some even say
That moms were once girls
So perhaps they're okay

Though boys are rather bear-like
A boy becomes a dad
So to be absolutely fair-like
Boys can't be all bad

Yes, it is rumored
And there are reports
Of girls good-humored
Girls good-sports

Oh, it's horrible how they harass you
Terrorize you, whine
And it's ridiculous how they sass you
But girls can be fine

Yes, there are rumors of boys
Who are excellent at sharing
Who will let you play with their toys
Who are affectionate and caring

Oh, it's awful how they spy
And wildly exaggerate
And, unlike girls, outright lie
Yet now and then boys are great

They're fine for summer swimming
They're fine for sports events
They're fine for jungle gym'ing
They're fine for forts 'n' tents

They're great to push 'n' wrassle
They're great for running races
For building a cushion castle
For making silly faces

Some appreciate snakes
Some appreciate flies
Oh, for goodness' sakes
Girls are one of the guys

Some appreciate zombies
Some appreciate drums
Oh, by golly wombies
Boys make excellent chums

Girls are trusting
Girls are wondrous
Girls are disgusting
Girls are thunderous

Boys are sensible
And now and then charming
They're incomprehensible
Boys are alarming

They're smiley, they're wily
They're highly crocodiley
But nothing can give your head swirls
Like those drastic, elastic
(Sometimes sarcastic)
Fantastic, fantastic GIRLS!

They're mysterious, serious
Can drive you delirious
But nothing brings joys or annoys
Like those curious, furious
(Sometimes uproarious)
Glorious, glorious BOYS!